Missy's
Life as a Slave

SAM PEMBERTON

Publishing Coordinator – Sharon Kizziah-Holmes
Cover Artist – Sandi Lemarr

Paperback-Press
an imprint of A & S Publishing
Paperback Press, LLC
Springfield, Missouri

ISBN -13: 978-1-960499-64-6

ACKNOWLEDGEMENTS

A special thanks to Sharon Kizziah Holmes, publishing coordinator, L. Kennedy, proofreader and Nancy B. Dailey, editor.

Nancy lost her battle with ALS while she was editing "Missy's life as a slave". She completed most of the work and furnished me with a list of questions she wanted answered. I spent my time considering each of her recommendations and made every effort to accomplish what she wanted.

I hope the book reflects what she had in mind. Nancy B Dailey will always be remembered for the way she treated me while she was doing the editing on all of the books I asked her to work on. RIP Nancy.

PREFACE

"Missy's Life as a Slave" is my best attempt to portray the effect of slavery on human relationships. The story begins with Missy's birth to an African mother and a Choctaw father. It continues with the relationships formed between her and the plantation owner's son.

They were raised together from the time Missy was born, and she developed a natural attraction to Caleb Matthews. Their relationship resulted in the birth of two children. Zeek and Ross were born with a white father and a half black and half Choctaw mother.

Donald Matthews and his wife, Francis, were typical plantation owners and were taken by surprise when they discovered they were the grandparents of two boys with questionable parentage. The story unfolds as they attempt to hide their son's role in fathering the two children.

As the story progresses, the relationship between the mistress of the plantation and the mother of her grandchildren evolves with the owner's need for companionship with her children. She lets Missy become her daughter by proxy and the fact she mothered "the boys".

The story details the loss of the children when they are removed to avoid embarrassment and follows the attempts to correct the problem.

The owners of the plantation change their attitude during the course of the story. They gained respect for Missy as she developed her talents in spite of being a slave and a cook.

I hope you can follow the emotional side of the story and see the changes that took place from the early 1800s until after the Civil War.

Also, I invite you to read my other stories, "Moonshiner and the Preacher", "Finding Big Flat", and "Zeek's Journey to Freedom". The stories, tied together, bring a closer picture of the lives of our forefathers as they faced the challenges of their day, and I hope it gives us a better understanding of the same challenges that still exist.

CHAPTER 1

S pring arrived in central Alabama. March came in like a lamb, rather than a lion. The warm, sunny days brought changes to the leaves of the live oak trees. A lighter green spring foliage replaced the darker green of winter.

A gentle breeze flowed through the trees as Missy walked toward the plantation kitchen. Missy, a slave owned by the Matthews family, was close to five and a half feet tall. Her mother was black and her father was a Choctaw. Her mother, also a slave, was a cook in the kitchen when Missy was born. Missy was beautiful, with a dark complexion and smooth skin with a coppery tint. Her eyes were a dark brown, with long lashes accenting the beautiful color. She had a well-rounded figure but appeared to be taller than she was.

She had started her walk to the kitchen from her living quarters. She walked at a leisurely pace, carrying herself with pride. She saw Donald Matthews, her owner, as he stopped his carriage in front of the main house. After Donald Matthews got out of the carriage, the driver took it to the shed and put the horses in their stalls.

She had not seen Donald Matthews for several days.

Mrs. Matthews was waiting for her in the kitchen. She asked Missy to make a spice cake for dinner. Spice cake was their favorite dessert. Mrs. Matthews then took the tray with tea cups and tea, and left the kitchen.

Missy wondered why Mrs. Matthews had not asked her to bring the tea to the house. It was also later than usual for tea. They usually had tea between three and four o'clock each afternoon.

Missy prepared to make the spice cake. She gathered the ingredients for the cake and took them to the table next to the parlor. She placed the dry ingredients into the mixing bowl and began to stir them together. She had just started mixing the flour and spices when she heard the Matthews family come into the parlor.

Why were they having their afternoon tea in the parlor? It was close to her, and she could hear them while she mixed the ingredients for the cake. As she listened, she decided she knew the answer.

They wanted her to hear their conversation.

"How was your trip to Mobile?" Mrs. Matthews asked.

Donald Matthews had gone to Mobile to get paid for the cotton crop. All of the cotton shipments had been completed in February, and this was his usual trip to collect payment for the crop. The cotton exchange paid for the entire season in a single payment.

"It was a good trip," he answered. He added, with no emotion, "I saw Joseph Reynolds."

Missy heard the name, but it meant nothing to her until Mrs. Matthews replied.

"Did he tell you anything about Zeek and Ross?" she asked.

Missy stopped stirring the sugar and cinnamon into the flour when she heard the names of the boys. Zeek and Ross were her sons. She was their mother, and Caleb Matthews, the son of Donald and Mrs. Matthews, was their father. Her mind flashed back to the day Donald Matthews had sent Caleb away because of the boys.

Her worst day ever followed a few years later when Donald Matthews removed the boys from the plantation.

Missy had been born on the plantation, into slavery, and because of that she was property of the plantation—the property of Donald Matthews—she had no rights. She could not make any demands. She had no input into any decision about herself or her children. She had no choice…about anything. Missy's life had always been as a slave.

After the boys had been taken away from her, Missy had written Caleb a letter. She found the address on Mrs. Matthews' desk, on a letter she had received from Caleb. She knew the boys had been sold as slaves. She had not known they had been sold to a plantation owner whom Mr. Matthews was acquainted with. Caleb never replied to her letter.

A few years after mailing the letter, Caleb had come for a visit. She only spoke to him briefly in the presence of his mother. No meaningful conversation occurred.

Missy had finished blending the dry ingredients by the time Donald Matthews replied to his wife's question.

"Yes, he told me about the boys," he answered.

Missy tried to stir the liquid into the cake batter as quietly as possible, so she could listen. It seemed to be forever before he spoke again.

"He let them join a survey crew, and they are somewhere in Arkansas," he said.

Missy had no idea what a survey crew was. She didn't know what joining a survey crew meant. She kept adding ingredients to the cake batter while trying not to get caught listening to the conversation.

"Did he tell you anything about them?" Mrs. Matthews asked with no emotion. It would have been hard to figure out she was talking about her grandchildren.

Missy finished adding the mixture of milk and juices to the dry flour and the other ingredients. This recipe was her re-creation of one she had learned from her mother years before. She was asked to make it for the Matthews family if they had a special occasion. She needed to stir the batter briskly and did so, hoping she could still hear the conversation in the next room.

Donald Matthews' voice was deep and easily heard.

"Yes, he did." Donald paused, then continued to tell the story of their grandchildren.

"Zeek is over six-foot tall, and is a muscular young man. Ross is a little bit shorter, and he still follows Zeek around."

Mrs. Matthews continued to ask questions because she wanted more of a description of the boys. She asked how much they had changed in appearance.

"What did they end up looking like?" she asked, referring to the fact that they left the plantation before they were ten years old.

"They must be a good-looking pair of young men," Mr. Matthews answered as he completed the story by telling how Joseph Reynolds went on and on about all the things they were able to do. He told about how the survey engineer, when he was selecting laborers for the survey crew, was almost finished, and then he saw Zeek and Ross working in the maintenance shed.

"Joseph said that when the engineer saw the boys, he immediately stopped and went over to where they were working."

Mrs. Matthews did not interrupt, but she was leaning toward her husband in anxious anticipation as he went on with his description of Zeek and Ross when they were selected for the survey crew.

"Joe asked if I thought he had violated our agreement." He was quiet after saying that.

"He was to never mistreat them, and he was never to give any indication that he knew who they were." The conversation ended.

Missy kept listening, but they never said anything else. She finished the cake batter and put it into the pans for baking.

Realizing there was not going to be any further discussion of the boys, Missy placed the cake in the oven and returned to her quarters while it was baking. She was left with her thoughts and memories of the boys.

CHAPTER 2

Missy reached her quarters. While it was still too early for bed, but she got ready as usual. The afternoon sun was shining into her room, as the days were getting longer in March. She would never go to bed this long before sundown. She would spend her time cleaning her quarters and doing laundry.

While she was dressed for bed, she laid down but was not able to go to sleep. Her thoughts were cluttered. She tried to sort out the discussion she heard between Mr. and Mrs. Matthews. As she lay thinking, she was trying to remember the boys. She tried to visualize what they would look like as young men. She could not imagine them being over six feet tall. She drifted off to sleep.

Missy usually dreamed about Caleb before he was sent away to college in New Hampshire. He was sent to Dartmouth, to get him away from Missy and the boys. She never understood the embarrassment they feared the boys would bring to the Matthews Plantation. She had no concept of what proper behavior for a young woman and her master's son should have been.

Tonight's dream was different. She was probably five years old in the dream. Caleb was just older than she was. They were playing in the dirt underneath the live oak tree. In the dream, it was about the same time of year in March. The dream was at least twenty years ago. Dreams never make any sense.

It started out when they were children playing in the dirt. Caleb put dirt down the back of her dress and he ran off. She jumped up to chase him.

When she caught up with him, they were laughing and fell to the ground. The dream turned into a memory. She skipped forward in the dream to when they discovered a passionate love for each other behind the toolshed.

Missy woke up crying. She was asking Caleb what went wrong. In the dream he assured her they would be fine.

After all these years, the memory of when they were childhood playmates before they became lovers and parents still lingered very clearly in Missy's mind. The memory became tainted when

Caleb was sent away to hide the shame of a plantation owner's son fathering two sons with a slave. The memory was very painful to Missy.

She was now wide awake and had stopped crying. She made her way to the kitchen and started her daily routine. She always prepared breakfast for the Matthews and took it to them on the veranda. If it was warm enough, they liked to eat outside.

She didn't know if they could tell she had been crying most of the night while she tried to decipher the dream and reconcile it with reality. She also was trying to understand what she had heard the day before.

"Missy, are you okay?" Donald Matthews seldom addressed her directly.

Shocked, Missy paused before she answered. "Yeah."

"I talked to the plantation owner where Zeek and Ross have grown up," Donald Matthews said, without a plan for what he was going to say next. "Missy, I have made a terrible mistake." Missy's hands were shaking as she set the breakfast in front of Mrs. Matthews. She looked down at the food with no expression. She could not look into the face of Donald Matthews after realizing he just admitted he might have made a big mistake by sending the boys away. Missy quickly looked up at him.

After exchanging glances with Missy, he started eating his breakfast.

"What's past…" He stopped in mid-thought. "What's past is past," he said, while continuing to eat his breakfast.

Missy went back to the kitchen and prepared to cook the bread for the day. She was responsible for cooking enough bread to feed everyone on the plantation. She would have a busy day with her work, but her thoughts would continue to be somewhere else.

She continued thinking about when she and Caleb would discuss their situation before he was sent away to college.

"Missy, there is no talking with dad about the boys." She remembered Caleb saying that continuously as they were searching for an answer.

She thought about her life as a slave. She was the daughter of a third-generation slave and she was trained in household duties. It was a privilege to not have to work in the fields. She enjoyed working in the kitchen. It was much easier work to cook and do laundry than labor in the hot sun of Alabama.

She recalled the discussions with her mother after she heard who her father was. He was a Choctaw man who came to the plantation to bring meat for the kitchen. Missy didn't know any of the details about her mother and her Choctaw father's relationship. When she became pregnant with Caleb's child, her mother questioned her, wondering if the father was a Choctaw man.

"Me and Caleb—" She started to tell her

mother, but stopped before she told her about their relationship.

Donald Matthews' words, "I have made a terrible mistake," continued to echo through her mind while she mixed the batter for the bread.

After she became pregnant there was absolutely no solution to hers and Caleb's situation, or any way to change the lives their sons were forced to live. Missy was still the property of the Matthews Plantation. Donald Matthews was her owner. He also owned her children. He gave no consideration to the fact Caleb was the father of Ross and Zeek. While they searched for a solution, neither she nor Caleb came up with an idea that would work.

She remembered the letter she wrote to Caleb just after the boys were taken away. She finished mixing the batter for the bread and placed it in the pans to rise before baking. She went back to her quarters and started a search for the address she had used to mail Caleb's letter years earlier. While she was searching, she realized he had moved and the address would not work.

"Dear Caleb," she looked at the scribbling as she began to write a new letter. She stopped. What need was there to write if she didn't have an address? She didn't have an answer. She was going to write her feelings to Caleb. He had come to visit a couple of years earlier, and she wasn't allowed to see him.

Missy laid the pencil down. She thought about the time while Caleb was visiting. "I only got a glimpse of him as he drove away in the buggy," she said aloud as she put the pencil and paper away.

CHAPTER 3

Missy stopped trying to write to Caleb and watched as the evening shadows were replaced by sunlight underneath the live oak tree.

Her memory went back to the first time she ever tried to make letters in the dirt. Caleb was helping her.

The memories of her first letters being formed in the sand with Caleb's help flashed through her mind as she watched the sunshine brighter underneath the tree and the shadows move away. The bright sunshine on the spot where they always sat with brought back more memories from those days.

When they were children, Caleb was taught to

read by tutor. She was probably three years old when the tutor would come to give him lessons. She would stand in the corner of the room watching and listening while the teacher taught him to make his letters and to read. While listening to the lesson she was also anxious for it to end so they could go back to playing underneath the tree.

"Caleb, I don't want to write anymore" she remembered saying.

"But Missy you need to learn this" he would insist until he was sure he had shared all of the last lesson.

Caleb chose a spot underneath the tree where the dirt was a mixture of sand and black loam to continue practicing the letters from the last lesson. Neither one of them realized why Missy was not being taught to read and write at the same time he was.

When she started cooking and needed to read the recipe book, she never let on to Mrs. Matthews she knew anything. The lessons she learned in the dirt while playing with Caleb allowed her to begin reading the recipe books. Since then, she had wondered if Mrs. Matthews realized Caleb spent the time after his lessons trying to teach her to write letters and read.

She remembered the day Caleb took her hand and tried to help her shape letters in the sand.

"Missy, that's a good job" she remembered him saying after she was able to write Missy.

"That's your name" the sound of his voice

seemed real as she remembered.

"What year was that? And how old were we when it happened?" The questions raced through her mind.

She also recalled how they continued to play in the dirt even after they began their relationship.

"Missy loves Caleb" with a heart drawn around it. She learned to write that and to draw the heart after Caleb had written: "Caleb loves Missy"

A smile came to her face when she remembered Caleb suddenly jerking her forward over the writing they had just finished. She was laying on top of the letters when she looked up into the face of Mrs. Matthews. Caleb was hiding the letters from his mother.

She often questioned her memories of their lives.

"How did the Matthews, her owners and Caleb's parents, allow them to become involved and have children?" The answer was not hers to figure out. Slavery produced unusual circumstances. Caleb and Missy's lives are a good example.

She was lost in memories of their relationship. The latch string for the door of her sleeping quarters was part of her memory.

A string running through the door to the outside. If you left the latch string out, a person could pull the latch up and enter the room. Missy would leave the string out when Caleb was planning on sneaking into her quarters. Her mind went back to the shed where the excess cloth was stored. The shed was another place where they continued their relationship before the boys were born.

How to write letters after all these years? There was no concept of right or wrong in Missy's mind. While she had learned a lot over the years, starting with listening in the corner while Caleb was being tutored. It was still a struggle with communication when the time came to use a pencil and paper.

While struggling to put words on paper, it was a difficult task to manage her thoughts at the same time. When she was able to think of what she wanted to say, by the time she tried to write it, it was too long for her to keep her train of thought. Writing the letters to Caleb since he left had improved her penmanship. While the first letter she wrote was the most difficult, the second letter after the boys were taken away was the easiest. It was easier because her thoughts were so strong. She had no trouble remembering what she wanted to say.

But today, she was confused by what she had learned. It was hard to realize enough time had passed for Zeke and Ross to be grown men. They were in Arkansas. She had no idea where that was. She also did not have any concept of them being members of a survey crew.

Just trying to cope with life was a great task and tested Missy's abilities. How could she write a letter to Caleb? She was still depressed but not as bad as it was when the boys were taken away.

With a pencil in her hand and tears in her eyes

with a mind that was trying to sort through what she had learned about the boys it was all too much for her to put on paper.

She turned away from the window. She went back to where the pencil lay on the paper. She did not pick it up.

Her memories had interrupted her and they were too strong for her to focus and try to write.

She would move forward with whatever opportunities that came up whatever they happen to be.

CHAPTER 4

After thinking about what she would like to say to Caleb, she retrieved the pencil and paper and started writing again. She would write another letter with hopes of obtaining Caleb's new address.

She recalled the things she had learned about Caleb since he left the plantation. She knew he had a wife. She knew they had children. The thoughts were hurtful and she stopped thinking about Caleb and thought of who she was.

"I am still the property of the Matthews Plantation." The thought never left her mind. While some of the other slaves her age was asked or told to have children with the slave chosen to be the father, Missy was not asked to have any more.

Donald Matthews always selected the pairing of the parents of the slaves to be born. She only wanted to be the mother of Zeek and Ross, and never thought of herself as the mother of other slaves.

Some of the women griped when they were asked to have children. Most of the women were anxious to have children because it meant they wouldn't have to work in the fields. While Missy did not understand the system of slavery, she knew it was a matter of pride to have special treatment during the time of the woman's pregnancy.

Missy learned over the years that Mrs. Matthews was deeply religious. She was a Presbyterian and considered the treatment of Ross and Zeek a mistake before Mr. Matthews ever admitted it. Missy's attitude toward Mrs. Matthews was changing. She didn't understand what the change was, but it seemed Mrs. Matthews was treating her differently. There seemed to be a mutual respect developing.

Missy remembered listening to her mother and Mrs. Matthews while they discussed their religious beliefs. Her thoughts returned to the letter she had decided to write.

She thought about Caleb, and what he told her before he left, "It's impossible for me to reconcile who we are as long as you are a slave and I am free—and the son of your owner."

Her thoughts interrupted her while she was trying to compose the letter. She was holding the pencil in her hand and staring at a blank sheet of paper.

Finally, she decided to just write her thoughts about the discussion with Caleb's parents.

"Your dad said he thought he made a terrible mistake taking the boys away." She looked at the scribbling after she wrote that, wondering if Caleb would be able to read it, if she ever got an address for him. After looking at it for a few minutes, she realized it looked better than when she wrote the letter telling Caleb about the boys leaving the plantation.

"I heard your dad telling your mother about the boys." She decided to just write the story as she heard it.

"He saw the owner of the plantation where Zeek and Ross have been living." Missy stopped. She was trying to remember exactly what Donald Matthews said.

"They are not there anymore," she wrote, and then stopped again. She became confused, trying to remember what the boys were doing.

She folded the letter with very few lines written and placed it underneath the bedding where she slept. Most of the paperwork she accumulated was hidden underneath her mattress, along with a picture of Caleb when he was a boy. She didn't know who the artist was that drew the picture. She had taken it when she found it laying on Mrs. Matthews' desk. She also had another drawing of her and Caleb when they were about five or six years old. She didn't know who the artist was of that picture either. She had gotten the second picture from the same place. She wondered if Mrs. Matthews left them for her intentionally. She loved to look at both drawings. The one with her and Caleb was drawn with them playing underneath the live oak tree between her sleeping quarters and the veranda of the main house.

She went to the door and looked toward the live oak tree. She tried to visualize the day the artist might have drawn the picture. Her memory of those days was still strong. Those memories confused her even more, and she would never understand slavery.

She enjoyed the freedom with Caleb while they were children. But after the boys were born and they had to keep out of sight, Missy did not understand the reason for Caleb being sent away. That memory hurt her too much to even think about. Life changed after he was sent away.

"We will do something when we have to," Caleb said repeatedly up until the time he left. They never came up with a plan for the boys or for their lives on the plantation.

Missy tried to remember how old she was when Caleb left. Her mother kept records of the summers. She had been seventeen years old. Seventeen summers she spent with Caleb before he was sent away. She was allowed six more summers with the boys before they were taken away.

She was now thirty years old. Her mother no longer worked in the kitchen. Her health had failed her, and she was living in a building reserved for the care of slaves at the end of their lives. Missy had taken over the cooking for the Matthews family. She cooked bread for the entire plantation, but most of her time was spent with Mrs. Matthews and preparing meals for the immediate family.

After Caleb left from his most recent visit, Missy knew she was sent away to do other things while he was there. She spent most of her time in the big kitchen helping the cook for all the slaves and to reorganize the kitchen where the slaves ate. It was the time when she barely caught a glimpse of him as he was leaving.

Once again, she decided to continue writing. She retrieved the paper and placed it back on the table. She was going to write a letter.

"Caleb, I don't have a calendar," she wrote. "I know what they are because there is one hanging in the main cook room."

She stopped again, trying to think of how to write about something she didn't understand. She had lost track of time and didn't know how much time had passed since the boys were taken away. She knew from the description Donald Matthews was given by the plantation owner that they were grown men.

"I believe Zeek may be seventeen years old," she wrote. "Zeek is the age I was when you left."

Once again, Missy stopped. Her limited education and lack of understanding about time and when events occurred made this difficult. There were too many things for her to understand about the years gone by for her to write about them in a letter.

It had been easy to write the letter after Mr. Matthews took the boys away. It was also easy to write about how much she missed Caleb.

Now it was different. She was still looking toward the live oak tree.

"Caleb, I hope you're happy." She spoke barely above a whisper. She was not going to retrieve the paper and start writing again.

The shadows underneath the live oak tree were gone, replaced with sunlight shining across the ground. It was where her life had begun with Caleb. The only shadow left was the trunk of the large oak tree. The shadow of the trunk stood out in the sunlight, accenting the place where they had played as children. This time of day meant a lot to Missy, and the spot under the oak tree was very special in her memory.

Missy was watching while the shadows underneath the oak tree were taken away by the sunlight. They were replaced by the bright evening sun. They had moved on. Caleb had moved on. He was living in Philadelphia. Missy had learned the boys were grown men. They were okay.

She was still a slave, owned by the Matthews Plantation.

SAM PEMBERTON

CHAPTER 5

Missy finished writing the letter to Caleb. She slept soundly with no dreams. She got up early and started her day. She crossed through the shadows of the live oak tree. She went up on the veranda. She was going through the parlor on her way to the kitchen. She didn't have a good reason for changing her usual route. Her thoughts were still lingering from the night before.

As she was going through the parlor, she stopped and looked into a mirror. She didn't usually look at herself. She was usually too depressed to care about her looks. In times past, she would make comparisons with her reflection in the mirror and others on the plantation. She knew she was short. She knew her hair was different from other slaves. She inherited straight hair from her Choctaw father.

As she looked at her reflection, she tried to imagine what Caleb saw when he looked at her. She wondered how he saw her when they were together and the boys were born. She wondered if he could still be attracted to her. She had seen pictures of Caleb and his new wife. His new wife appeared to be tall and slim, a white woman.

She left the parlor and went into the office. She went to Mrs. Matthews' desk and began looking for a cookbook. She was starting the search for it when she opened the third drawer on the right side of the desk. She was looking through some papers and discovered they were letters from Caleb. She remembered she had seen Mrs. Matthews leave earlier in the day with Mr. Matthews.

Missy began to read. She did not feel guilty reading the letters Caleb had written to his mother. She did not have a sense that it was wrong to read the letters. She had never considered she would be able to read them before.

"I am busy..." Missy read a description of one of Caleb's days as an attorney. She didn't understand any of the writing about his activity.

She continued reading until she read, "...and Missy is all right and still doing the cooking?"

She stopped reading that letter and continued rummaging through the papers until she found another letter from Caleb.

"Mother, I want to be back this summer—the heat bothered Charlotte too badly for us to come again in July." Caleb had written a long description of all the things that his wife and children hated about summer in Alabama. "We have a cabin in the mountains north of Philadelphia and we will spend our vacation time there, if we have any." Missy quit reading and went to the kitchen. She started organizing all the recipes she had written down from the cookbook she had been searching for. Her mother taught her to copy the recipes and cook from the copies rather than trying to keep the cookbook in the area of the stove. It was very easy to ruin a cookbook if something went wrong. It only took one time with a grease fire for Missy to understand her mother's instructions.

When Mrs. Matthews brought the cookbook back from Europe, it became necessary for Missy to be able to read. As Mrs. Matthews read the instructions to Missy, she followed along in the book and learned to read without realizing it. As Missy learned to read and write, she also developed an affection for Mrs. Matthews. Missy's reading and writing improved over the years. She was gaining an education. The instructions in the cookbook required the measuring of ingredients, and became a math lesson in disguise.

The more Missy learned, the more she was able to learn. She began to read everything available to her after she learned to read and copy the recipes from the cookbook. Her writing, her math, and her understanding of what she read were all developed from trying to translate the cookbook into things she understood.

As Missy's reading and writing improved, she was able to use what she learned to communicate better about other things, as well.

CHAPTER 6

The year was 1820. Missy made a lot of progress as a person, considering the time she lost when she was so depressed after losing Caleb and then the boys. She never gave up on life. She was starting to learn a lot of things and was developing a desire to become free. She had no idea how to do it.

Missy was exposed to all of the beliefs of the Matthews family. The time she spent cooking and serving them tea on the veranda was filled with discussion of all their beliefs and ideas. They were of the Presbyterian faith. Missy's religious beliefs were rooted in the traditional African religions still practiced by the slaves on the plantation.

After Missy learned to read, she began reading

everything she could find on religion, Dartmouth College, and slavery and why it should end. The writings of a minister from Dartmouth were very supportive of freedom and he openly stated in one of his writings, "slavery must end."

Missy did not know where Caleb went to law school. She knew it was in New York City. Like Philadelphia, the name "New York" meant nothing to Missy. Her world was limited to the Matthews Plantation in Alabama.

While her world was limited, she was expanding it by reading everything available to her. Missy continued to read Caleb's letters. Any time Mrs. Matthews was gone, she found time to snoop through her desk and look for them. Missy's curiosity about Caleb was never satisfied. She wondered continually about his life. She had no way of sending him the letters she was writing. She wrote and told him about Zeek and Ross working on the survey crew. While her letters remained un-mailed, she continued to write about everything she knew.

She gave up looking for the cookbook and went to work in the kitchen.

"Have you seen anybody in my office?" Mrs. Matthews asked Missy when she returned.

"I was in there looking for the old cookbook, but I didn't find it," Missy answered. She did not blush, nor was she afraid to answer.

"Oh, Missy, I should've told you, I loaned the old cookbook to a lady at church," Mrs. Matthews answered apologetically.

Missy felt relieved, and she was not worried about Mrs. Matthews knowing she had gone through the desk.

CHAPTER 7

Missy became more curious about Caleb's life each time she read one of his letters. She read several over the next few months.

She overheard Mrs. Matthews tell Donald she would be glad to ride to the next plantation and spend the day with a neighbor. Missy made plans to go to the office while she was gone and read more of Caleb's letters.

Missy was shocked when she saw two letters tied together with ribbon and a note saying, "Missy, these are the last two letters I have gotten from Caleb!" Mrs. Matthews had written the note in large letters.

Missy's face flushed when she realized Mrs.

Matthews knew she was reading Caleb's letters. She untied the ribbon and opened the letters.

The first letter began with, "Mother, it's cold in Philadelphia this morning." Missy continued reading several pages of the letter before anything of interest to her was written. Her eyes bulged with surprise when she got to the last part of the letter. "The time for slavery is coming to an end," Caleb had written. He went on to explain how freedom was being gained as slaves became more educated and more aware of the fact they didn't have to stay in servitude. He listed the states where slavery was not allowed.

"It will come to an end," he had written. The next line shocked Missy the most: "I just wish it had been before my life ended with Missy and the boys." She read it twice more before she was convinced she had read it correctly the first time.

She held the letter against her while tears filled her eyes. She asked herself, "Why did Mrs. Matthews leave these letters for me to read?"

She returned the letters to the desk with the ribbon tied around them.

Missy's work went smoother than usual for the rest of the morning. She heard Mrs. Matthews return and enter the kitchen.

She didn't speak, but came over and stopped in front of Missy. She backed up a step and looked at Missy, as if she was inspecting her. Without saying a word she gave Missy a hug and left the kitchen.

While time had passed slowly since Caleb left,

neither Missy nor Mrs. Matthews realized their relationship was changing so much. Neither of them knew or even thought about the change. Missy became more than the cook, and Mrs. Matthews was no longer her master. Neither of them ever thought about the way they were filling a void. Mrs. Matthews wanted her to understand more about her life, including Caleb. Missy was depending on the letters to keep her informed. Missy finished her day and went to her quarters.

She decided she wanted to read all the letters she attempted to write Caleb and never mailed.

"Caleb," she wrote, beginning another letter, but nothing came to mind after writing his name. She didn't know how long she sat holding the pencil and looking at the paper. She seldom cried, but her mind would become a jumble of thoughts trying to make sense of the years.

Missy did not dream when she went to bed. She didn't go to sleep immediately, because one line Caleb had written continued to flow through her mind.

"I just wish it had been before my life ended with Missy and the boys."

The sun was shining brightly the next morning. It was one of those clear and cold winter days when Missy left her quarters to go to the kitchen. The sun came up with a red glow covering almost half of the sky. The reflection of the sun on the live oak tree seemed to put a tinge of gold around the edges of the leaves. Missy didn't stop to look at the ground beneath the tree. Not this morning. She didn't need any more memories cluttering up her thoughts.

Missy had cooked the breakfast meal and was cleaning the kitchen. She started to make the usual batches of bread and was waiting for Mrs. Matthews to request anything else she wanted cooked.

She was starting to mix the batter when Mrs. Matthews came into the kitchen.

"Missy, when you catch up with the bread, could you come and join me on the veranda?" Mrs. Matthews asked.

Missy did not answer. She thought it was too cold for them to sit on the veranda. When she left the kitchen with the tea and cups, she went through the parlor. She expected Mrs. Matthews to be waiting there. She was not. Missy went to the veranda. Missy listened to the tea service as the pitcher and cups rattled on the tray. She had never been nervous enough for them to rattle before.

Missy set the tea service down on the table next to the chair where Mrs. Matthews was sitting. She remained standing. Mrs. Matthews was looking at Missy as if to study her for the first time. Missy wasn't sure how long it was before she spoke.

"Missy, would you sit down and join me?" The words echoed on the veranda with meaning.

Missy looked at the live oak tree. She had been on the veranda many times when she would carry food or drink to Mr. and Mrs. Matthews. She had never taken the time to look back toward the kitchen and her living quarters. She was now seeing the view where Mrs. Matthews had watched her and Caleb as children. She thought of the times Mrs. Matthews must have watched as Zeek and Ross played underneath the big tree.

"Missy, you read the letters I left for you?" Mrs. Matthews asked.

Missy felt her face flush. She could feel the embarrassment, or maybe excitement, flooding her face.

"Yes, ma'am," she finally answered.

"I want you to be a part of my life, Missy." Mrs. Matthews made the statement without any emotion.

"What do you mean?" Missy asked.

Missy was always at the Matthews Plantation. It was where she was born. Mrs. Matthews had been there for every day of her life. She had worked in the kitchen since she was a child. She was the mother of Mrs. Matthews' grandsons, Zeek and Ross. Missy couldn't think of any way she could be any more a part of Mrs. Matthews life than she had been for all these years. She was waiting for the answer to her question.

"Caleb writes me polite letters. Letters that make him feel better. They are more like a report than a family letter." She paused, taking a sip from the tea before continuing. "I don't know what I mean, or what I expect from you, Missy." Mrs. Matthews paused again, and with a sigh, she added, "Donald is always busy with something."

Mrs. Matthews leaned back in her chair. "Missy, you're over thirty years old." She made the statement just as a matter of fact.

"I remember the morning you were born really well." Again, she paused and seemed to be studying the area around the live oak tree.

"You were the prettiest baby I had ever seen." A deep smile covered her face, and her eyes lit up when she added, "And Caleb was a second prettiest baby."

They sat silently. They sipped tea. There was a new understanding developing between them. Missy loved to rock in her chair. She was rocking with a slow rhythm, not enough to spill the tea or hard enough to disrupt her thoughts. She noticed Mrs. Matthews was rocking her chair in a rhythm with hers. They had achieved a common spirit and attitude.

"When I get a letter from Caleb—" Mrs. Matthews gestured toward Missy. "I'll always share it with you."

She didn't explain why she was going to share Caleb's letters. They continued to rock their chairs in rhythm and enjoyed the silence. Mrs. Matthews broke the silence after a few minutes.

"We will never let Caleb or Mr. Matthews know what we are doing," Mrs. Matthews said.

Missy was not sure how long they sat on the veranda. She didn't remember if there was any more conversation as she went back through the parlor with the tea set. She returned to her work in the kitchen.

CHAPTER 8

A lot of years passed after the day Mrs. Matthews asked Missy to sit with her on the veranda. She continued to place the letters from Caleb in the drawer for Missy to read. She also began placing newspapers in the same drawer, along with a suggestion of what article she would like for Missy to read.

Missy's knowledge became broader as she read the newspapers and Caleb's letters. However, the conversations with Mrs. Matthews were never about anything other than Caleb and the boys in the beginning. She loved to talk about when they were still living on the plantation.

From the date lines on the newspaper, Missy realized it was the late 1840s. She was past fifty years old, and Mrs. Matthews was approaching seventy. Their relationship had reached a point where they were comforting each other. Mrs. Matthews would always tell her when Caleb and his wife were coming to visit.

Missy always found something else to do while Caleb was at the plantation. She would accompany supplies being delivered to the other properties on the plantation. She was avoiding seeing Caleb. She would always stay until after she was sure he'd gone back to Philadelphia.

She continued to grow closer to Mrs. Matthews over the years. A relationship which started out as a relationship between an owner and her slave turned in to a mother-daughter's relationship. Missy's mother passed away in the late spring of 1843. Mrs. Matthews insisted she be buried in the family plot, rather than the area where all the other slaves had been buried for over a hundred years previously.

When Mrs. Matthews would make a trip to Mobile, she always brought Missy something new. When she brought a new dress to Missy, she made sure she liked it before she gave it to her.

Mrs. Matthews never discussed Caleb's wife. She never referred to Charlotte as her daughter-in-law. She would not discuss Caleb and Charlotte's children. She ignored the fact she had grandchildren with Charlotte as their mother. Missy would not ask any questions about Mrs.

Matthews' relationship with Caleb or his family.

"Glad we are back to normal," was Mrs. Matthews' usual comment after each of Caleb's visits. She always wanted Missy to come to the veranda as soon as they were gone. She just didn't think of Charlotte as being part of the family.

She liked to discuss her daughters with Missy. The Matthews family insisted their two daughters go to Europe to complete their education. They went and seldom returned. If they did return, it was for a very short visit. One of them lived in France with her family, and Missy couldn't remember where the other daughter lived. It was somewhere in Europe.

One day, after discussing the daughters and their children Missy asked, "What are the children's names?"

Mrs. Matthews laughed. "Missy, this is pitiful," she said, stopping and taking a drink of her tea before she laughed again. Then she answered Missy's question. "I don't know. I know I have four grandchildren who were born in Europe over the last thirty years." She paused as she tried to recall their names. "I even have great-grandchildren. The oldest great-grandchild's name is James. They live in England."

Mrs. Matthews began a long explanation about why they never came back to Alabama. She interrupted herself and said, "Missy, we don't need to talk about them."

She sat quietly for a while. She picked up the subject again and said, "I have no idea what happened between us and our children." She paused again before adding, "We just became alienated from each other, and lost touch."

She started a description of her life and the life she had lived with Donald Matthews. Donald Matthews was the son of a wealthy planter. She had been Francis Cabot, and was living in Boston when they met. The Matthews family got the plantation in Alabama, early on, when it was being settled. Donald's family had residences in Charleston, South Carolina, and Boston, Massachusetts. When they got married, the family suggested that Donald should take the plantation in Alabama. The idea seemed exciting to the young Matthews couple. Mrs. Matthews continued to tell the story and showed more excitement as she told details of them moving to Alabama.

"I enjoyed the early years when we were developing land and building the buildings," she said.

Then she admitted a lot of the work was done several years before she and Donald were married. She never mentioned slavery or how many slaves were living on the plantation when they arrived. Mrs. Matthews never talked about the slaves.

Missy had listened intently as she told the story. "Do you remember when my mother came to the plantation?" Missy asked.

"Yes," she answered quickly. "I definitely

remember your mother, she was always neat and I wanted her to work in the kitchen, the same one where you work, close to the house."

Missy did not ask about her father, but Mrs. Matthews sensed the question, and the look on Missy's face caused Mrs. Matthews to volunteer the story of her father.

"I never realized the Choctaw Indian who brought the meat to the kitchen was seeing your mother." It was the only explanation she gave before she added, "He was a charming young man. It was easy to see why your mother—" she stopped mid-sentence and didn't explain any further.

They sat in silence after this discussion and didn't return to either subject.

Missy left the veranda without knowing why the Matthews children in Europe never visited the plantation. She also knew Caleb's visits got shorter and spaced wider apart the longer he was gone.

Missy continued to read all the newspapers. Mrs. Matthews would leave a copy of *The Boston Globe* or *The Philadelphia Inquirer* on her desk almost weekly.

After she would leave a newspaper, she would give Missy enough time to know she had read them and then she would ask Missy about the things in it. It made their visits more interesting as they developed a dialogue about current events. Without even realizing it, they were beginning to follow the objections to slavery. They were following the divisions in the country between the free states and the slave states.

The Missouri Compromise in 1840, when Maine came in as a free state and Missouri came in as a slave state, actually started the discussions about the disputes they were following in the newspapers.

Missy wondered if Mrs. Matthews, by giving her access to information and treating her almost as an equal, was giving her freedom. Their relationship was changing and entering a new phase constantly. The discussions were allowing Missy to learn and develop an opinion unavailable to almost anyone in slavery.

"Or is it because I am Zeek and Ross's mother?", was a question Missy asked herself on several occasions.

All of these conversations started after Donald Matthews said he thought he made a mistake when he removed Zeek and Ross from the plantation.

Missy was starting to get acquainted with Donald Matthews, also. He would sit on the veranda with them. She would serve the tea and neither she nor Mrs. Matthews ever mentioned anything about their discussions to him. He seemed to be developing a different attitude toward Missy—almost as much change as Mrs. Matthews. He was becoming mellow. He was no longer robust and energetic in the management of the plantation. He trained two slaves to assist him, along with a nephew who came to visit one summer and stayed over. Missy knew the name of his nephew, James, but he never addressed Missy directly when he was in her presence.

Missy was reading a lot. The more she read, the more she learned about slavery, and her future became more uncertain. She was curious about what would happen if she suddenly became a free woman. She decided to ask Mrs. Matthews.

"What happens to me, if one day you don't own me?" she finally asked Mrs. Matthews one afternoon when they sat down for tea.

"Missy, I decided many years ago you already have your freedom." Mrs. Matthews lifted her head and looked straight at Missy. Missy saw the emotion. There was a glaze in Mrs. Matthews' eyes, almost tears.

"I understand now why Caleb loved you, and I wish I could undo what has been done, but the best I can do is treat you—" she stopped.

They sat in silence while Missy waited for Mrs. Matthews to continue. She did not. Missy decided it was time for her to go back to the kitchen. She picked up the tea service as usual, but this time, she leaned over and gave Mrs. Matthews a hug.

CHAPTER 9

As Missy's and Mrs. Matthews' relationship developed, they continued to grow closer emotionally. Missy looked forward to sitting on the veranda with her. Their discussions of Ross and Zeek and Caleb were their favorite topics. Missy enjoyed their visits.

Afterwards, she would go home to her quarters and dig out the last letter she had written to Caleb. None of those were ever mailed. She would read them, reviewing what she had written before she wrote the next letter. They now covered a period of time longer than twenty years.

Since the start of her discussions with both of the Matthews', she was able to write more than, "Dear Caleb".

She read the pages filled with her feelings. It was becoming easier to write each time after she sat with Mrs. Matthews. She gave a lot of thought to who Mrs. Matthews had become to her. "She has become—" Missy stopped thinking and trying to describe Mrs. Matthews. After her mother died, she wondered if she had tried to replace her with Mrs. Matthews.

"Friends? No," Missy thought. "It's just different."

Her vocabulary didn't have enough words to describe her present position at the Matthews Plantation. She was still their property. Being someone else's property lacked meaning when Missy thought of her life. She had always been at the plantation. It was the only place she understood, where she was born, and where she had always lived. The kitchen and the living quarters where she slept were the extent of where she had been. Her world was very small in comparison to Caleb and the Matthews family.

Over the years, her living quarters had been remodeled. During the last few years, Mrs. Matthews instructed the plantation carpenters to expand Missy's bedroom into more than an area to sleep.

They extended the west side of the room. They created room for a desk and installed a window above it. They added enough room for more furniture. She now had a wardrobe closet for her clothes, along with a full-length mirror. Her desk had enough drawers to store a lot of paperwork, including the letters she had written to Caleb.

Of all the furniture, Missy's favorite was the wardrobe. It was a nice cabinet with room to hang all of her dresses along with drawers for storing her undergarments. Missy's wardrobe closet was full of clothes. In addition to the dresses, Mrs. Matthews was giving her shoes after she decided she didn't want to wear them anymore.

They discovered their feet were the same size when Mrs. Matthews kicked off her shoes on the veranda and then asked Missy if she would pick them up for her. When Missy reached down to get the shoes, Mrs. Matthews said, "Try that shoe on, Missy."

Missy hesitated. She was barefoot. She didn't put shoes on earlier. She liked to walk barefoot on the cool ground between the kitchen and her living quarters.

"My feet are dirty," she answered Mrs. Matthews.

"Don't matter, Missy," Mrs. Matthews said with a laugh. "Just put the shoe on."

Missy remembered Mrs. Matthews standing up to look down at her foot after she put the shoe on.

"Fits perfect," she said as she stood and looked down at Missy's foot. "Put the other one on, too," she said as she kicked the shoe over toward Missy.

Missy felt awkward walking away from the veranda wearing Mrs. Matthews' shoes.

When she pulled them off, she put them under

her bed. She had not worn them again before Mrs. Matthews brought her a new pair, along with the new dress.

"Missy, I don't want you wearing my hand-me-down clothes," she said before she handed her two boxes. "This pair of shoes and the dress are for you." She paused before adding, "They are brand-new."

While Missy's treatment continued to improve with all the new clothes she was receiving, she liked having access to Caleb's letters the most. She also enjoyed reading the letters she wrote to Caleb. She continued writing, despite knowing they would never be mailed. She wrote mostly about Caleb's mother asking questions neither one of them knew the answer to. She wrote about Mrs. Matthews' continual questions about Zeek and Ross.

"Do you think they would know us?" was the question Mrs. Matthews asked almost every day.

Missy never tried to answer the question. She had no idea. She barely remembered what the boys looked like the day Mr. Matthews took them away. She was crying as she watched their little faces trying to sneak a peek back toward her. She remembered Donald Matthews warning them not to look back.

Missy tried to remember the letter she wrote Caleb. She had mailed it to the address Mrs. Matthews left for her to find.

She remembered the day she finally asked Mrs.

Matthews if she left the address for her intentionally.

"Yes, I did," she answered firmly. "And I was thrilled the day Caleb told me he got your letter."

Missy went back to her quarters and was getting ready for bed as usual. She sat on the edge of her bed, silently thinking about why Mrs. Matthews wanted her to write Caleb.

"She must've wanted me to tell him the story about the boys leaving," she decided. After all the years since the letter she wrote Caleb, she finally realized he had known when the boys were taken away. She still wondered if Donald Matthews told his son about selling his grandchildren to another plantation owner. Missy also wondered if Mr. Matthews received any funds for the boys.

After spending some time reminiscing and reading old letters, Missy could make more sense of her relationship with Mrs. Matthews. She finished writing another letter to Caleb, knowing she would not mail it, either.

She went to bed and lay down without dreaming. She knew who she was. She was still living at the Matthews Plantation, and she could remember a lot of things she had tried to forget. She had no idea where life was heading, and she was not in control of planning her future, but she knew that she would make the best of it.

CHAPTER 10

November weather in Alabama could be the nicest time of year. It was one of those days. Missy got up before the break of dawn to start cooking bread for everyone on the plantation. She stayed busy all morning. When she was about to take her break, she heard someone coming into the kitchen. She had thought Mrs. Matthews was with Donald in Mobile, but she was wrong.

"Missy! Missy!" Mrs. Matthews was yelling for her. Missy stopped what she was doing and went to investigate.

She was not sure where Mrs. Matthews' voice was coming from. She started into the parlor and then realized it was coming from the outside. She turned and saw Mrs. Matthews standing at the end of the veranda next to the kitchen. She was waving something in the air. It was papers. She was holding them in her right hand, while she was yelling, "Missy!"

Missy started to go through the parlor and out to the veranda, but she decided to go outside on the ground. She made it to the end of the veranda before she answered Mrs. Matthews.

"Yes, ma'am?" she said—the answer she always used when answering Mrs. Matthews after she would call her name.

Mrs. Matthews had returned to the center of the veranda before she heard Missy answer. She came back to the end next to Missy and looked down at her. She was still holding the papers in her right hand, which she was still waving while she yelled for Missy.

"You need to bring some tea and come to the veranda, right now!" Mrs. Matthews was still excited.

Missy didn't try to hurry. She was taking her time as she returned to the kitchen. She was wondering what could be so urgent. They were drinking hot tea. She poured the tea from the pot into the serving pitcher. She placed two cups on the tray along with a few lumps of sugar. Her hands were steady as she carried the tray through the parlor and out onto the veranda.

"Come sit down," Mrs. Matthews was still excited, but now her voice was calm. "Pour us some tea," she said as she handed Caleb's letter to Missy, adding, "This is going to take us a while."

Missy laid the letter on the serving table before she started to pour the tea. She still had no idea why Mrs. Matthews was so excited. She poured the tea slowly making sure she left the room in Mrs. Matthews cup for the three lumps of sugar. She stirred the tea after adding the sugar and handed Mrs. Matthews her cup. She poured her tea adding the usual amount of sugar. She sat down and lifted her cup from the tray. She took a sip to make sure the two lumps of sugar were enough.

"You will want to put your tea back on the tray." Mrs. Matthews pointed to the tray. She had picked the letter up from the table and was holding a newspaper clipping with it. She handed both of them back to Missy.

"It will take us a while to read these." Mrs. Matthews waited for Missy to unfold the letter. Missy read the letter first. Mrs. Matthews was right. Caleb had written some exciting news.

After Caleb wrote his usual greeting, he wrote, "Mother, I just bought a train ticket to West Plains, Missouri."

Missy had never heard of West Plains, Missouri. She wondered why he was writing about a train trip to Missouri.

"I am going to Arkansas. I have sent a newspaper clipping from *The Philadelphia Inquirer*. After you read the article in the newspaper, you will understand why I am going."

The storyline in the newspaper was a report from Searcy County, Arkansas. The story was about a plantation owner trying to reclaim a runaway slave.

Missy stopped reading the letter and her eyes turned to the newspaper she was holding in her hand. She spent the next several minutes reading and rereading the newspaper article. She read a line that said "the key witness in the trial for the ownership of Zeek, a runaway slave, was his brother, Ross. His testimony left little doubt as to who Zeek was."

After reading the line for the third time, Missy was silent.

"Can you believe that?" she asked after a moment of thinking.

Mrs. Matthews returned the question. "Can *you* believe it?"

Missy didn't attempt to answer. She went back to reading Caleb's letter. She read the lines where he explained having to tell Charlotte him about Missy and the boys.

"Mother, it doesn't matter what she thinks. I am going to see my son. I am going to Arkansas to see Zeek," Caleb had written.

Neither Missy nor Mrs. Matthews knew how much time they spent on the veranda reading the letter and the newspaper article over several times. Their discussion had become a continuous flow of questions.

Missy had the most questions. She read in the newspaper article where a man named Mr. Hayes stopped the trial and paid the plantation owner for Zeek's freedom. She wondered how he had that much support from anyone. She read that he was a family man respected in the community. From reading the newspaper article, it appeared he was accepted for who he was with no one questioning his race.

Missy wondered where Searcy County, Arkansas was located. She tried to visualize the little boy in the wagon as he was taken from the plantation. She tried to visualize him as a grown man with a family. She couldn't do it.

"Are you going to tell Mr. Matthews?" she asked Mrs. Matthews.

Mrs. Matthews leaned back in her chair. She put her hands on the armrest, trying to stretch herself farther back into the chair. Her reading glasses slid down on her nose. She turned her head to face Missy as she peered over the glasses.

"I don't know," she finally answered.

Mrs. Matthews was trying to think of a way to tell Donald they had a grandson living in Arkansas who was now a free man. She couldn't think of a way to tell him about Caleb leaving Philadelphia to make the trip to see Zeek.

Mrs. Matthews had enjoyed the years of sharing her letters with Missy. The letters from Caleb were part of what allowed their relationship to develop. He gave them an understanding of each other.

Caleb's letters were their common bond.

They now had more in common than letters. Missy had a son. He was Zeek Matthews. He was living in Arkansas as a free man. Mrs. Matthews was a grandmother and she was also a great-grandmother.

Missy asked if she could keep the letter and the newspaper clipping.

"No," Mrs. Matthews answered strongly. She added, "Not until I give them to Donald and let him read all of this for himself."

She had made up her mind. She would let Donald Matthews know what their children and grandchildren were doing.

They left the veranda.

Tomorrow's discussion would have more details for sure.

CHAPTER 11

After reading the letter and newspaper clipping, Missy had a sleepless night. She couldn't get the letter or the newspaper article out of her mind. She had reread both of them constantly as they passed through her thoughts during the night.

She went to the kitchen early and began her daily routine of making bread. She had started stirring the batter when Donald Matthews came in. He watched as she stirred the flour.

He had never been in the kitchen with her before. He walked around her twice, stopping each time as if he was going to say something. He was making Missy nervous.

"When Mrs. Matthews comes in, I want you and

her to join me on the veranda," he said as he was turning to leave, adding, "I'll drink coffee this morning."

He left the kitchen. Missy placed the batter in the pans for baking and then she set them on the top of the stove where the bread would rise. It would be about an hour before the bread was ready to put in the oven. Missy's nerves did not calm down. She poured a cup of coffee and took it to Mr. Matthews on the veranda.

"Thanks, Missy." Donald Matthews was being unusually polite. "You come back with Mrs. Matthews as soon as she gets to the kitchen."

Mrs. Matthews came into the kitchen and was smiling when she greeted Missy. She stood for a minute before she said, "Come on with me, girl," as she walked away, before adding, "We've got to talk."

Missy followed Mrs. Matthews to the veranda. Donald had brought an extra chair and placed it at an angle in front of where he and Mrs. Matthews usually sat. He motioned for Missy to sit in the chair.

Missy sat down. She looked at Mrs. Matthews before she looked at Donald. Mrs. Matthews was still smiling and looked happy just as she had looked when she came into the kitchen. Missy looked at Mr. Matthews. He was serious and showed no signs of emotion.

"I read Caleb's letter." He had a slight smile. "I also read the newspaper article several times."

He stopped and drank a few sips of coffee. He was moving his eyes from Missy back to his wife, Caleb's mother. He did this for what seemed like forever to Missy, though it was actually only a few seconds. He had a look that indicated he was trying to think of what he was going to say next.

He was hesitant when he started to speak. "It's been a lot of years," he said with no indication of what he was referring to until he added, "Slavery is coming to an end." He looked at Missy and realized the statement was confusing to her.

He went on to explain in considerable detail how divided he thought the country was becoming. He said he was against the 1852 law that allowed plantation owners to reclaim their slaves. He stopped the discussion of slavery after he said that.

"I think I feel differently about the laws now." He stood up and walked to the edge of the veranda. He was looking at the ground beneath the live oak tree.

"We might never have known where Zeek is if it had not been for the trial in Arkansas." He was giving credit to a law he was against for providing the information which resulted in knowing where Zeek was living.

"Missy, I wanted you here this morning." Donald Matthews was finding it hard to express himself.

"We are getting old," he said, referring to himself and Mrs. Matthews. "You know our children. The girls seldom come back from

Europe." He went on to correct himself. "Seldom is the wrong word. They never come back from Europe. Caleb has not come back but a few times after he left for college."

He went on to explain that Charlotte, their daughter-in-law, despised Alabama.

"They have two children who have grown up in St. Louis." He seemed sad after making the statement. "They have never called me by any name other than Mr. Matthews."

Donald Matthews returned to his chair and sat back down once again facing Missy.

"I don't know what I've been trying to say." He stopped again in mid-thought and took another drink of his coffee. He laughed and interrupted himself. "We're going to have to switch to tea. This conversation is going to take a while."

Missy returned with the hot tea. She had to go back to the kitchen for the sugar.

"Mr. Matthews, I've never served you tea."

"I don't know if you take sugar in your tea or not," she said.

"I drink mine just like your mother-in-law." He paused and added, "Missy".

The comment took Missy by surprise. She had never thought of herself being anyone other than a slave owned by the plantation.

Her look of surprise caused Donald Matthews to continue his thought.

"You have treated us better than anyone else over the years," he said. "I wish you'd spoken up and protested years ago before I sent Caleb away, and especially before I took Ross and Zeek."

Missy sat down. Donald Matthews was right. The conversation was going places Missy had never considered, and she didn't know how to contribute.

"What can we do now?" he asked. It was an open question that he asked without expecting an answer.

Mrs. Matthews had sat silently all morning. She drank coffee but didn't finish the first cup. She hated the taste of it. After they switched to tea, she drank quite a bit, and listened intently as her husband was asking the questions and making his statements.

"I think we do nothing until we hear from Caleb after his visit to see Zeek," she said, entering the conversation. "I hope he writes a good letter telling us all about our grandson."

Missy still had not joined the conversation. She did not know how to interject any of her feelings into the conversation she recognized her status had changed from a slave. From a slave to what? She couldn't fill in the blank or answer the question.

According to Mr. Matthews, he considered her Mrs. Matthews' daughter-in-law. How could that be? They were ashamed to accept that she was the mother of Zeek and Ross. They sent Caleb away as soon as they realized it was going to become obvious to everyone on the plantation and to all the neighbors.

The live oak tree where Zeek and Ross spent most of their time playing was in clear sight of the area where they entertained the neighbors. They could not host their outside dinners without the boys being seen.

The live oak tree was the same place where Caleb and Misty spent most of their childhood. It was the oak tree where Missy started chasing Caleb around the toolshed after he put dirt down the back of her dress. The day she chased him and they caught up in a hug as they fell to the ground was the day their relationship changed.

Now, almost fifty years later, she was on the veranda listening to Mr. and Mrs. Matthews. Donald and Francis.

Missy left the veranda having listened to all the conversation, but still not knowing what to expect to happen next.

CHAPTER 12

Caleb's trip to see Zeek lasted almost a month. He left Philadelphia with a ticket on the train to West Plains, Missouri. He rented a horse and buggy in West Plains with instructions how to get to Cotter, Arkansas. He found the people helpful, giving him directions how to get to Searcy County. The return trip was easier because he knew the route back to West Plains, Missouri. He rode the train to St. Louis, but he didn't stop to see his and his wife's sons or his St. Louis in-laws.

He had too much on his mind after spending time with Zeek and meeting all of his grandchildren. He had enjoyed meeting Vida, Zeek's wife. She had treated him like royalty. He had discovered a whole new diet while he was visiting in Arkansas. He couldn't wait to get back to Alabama and share a recipe for dumplings. Vida had made them with all the meat she cooked during his visit. After the train left the station, he slept all night as he traveled back to Philadelphia.

When he reached the train station in Philadelphia, He hired a livery for the ride home. It was late. He sat his luggage by his desk and went to bed.

Caleb slept in the next morning, getting up much later than usual. He was tired, even after sleeping on the train. When he woke up and got dressed, he was sorting through the personal mail on the dining table when he found a note from Charlotte.

"Read the letter I left on your desk at the office." She had not signed her name, nor was anything else written on the note.

Caleb always walked to his office. This morning was no different. He enjoyed the walk along the street and in the bright sunshine. While it was the end of October and early November, the sun was still warm. The maple leaves in Arkansas, with their fall colors, were brighter than those along the streets of Philadelphia. Philadelphia had a lot of pretty trees, but Caleb's mind was not on the fall foliage.

He had walked slowly and made it to his office. His mind was beginning to clear as he started relating where he had been in Arkansas to where his life was in Philadelphia.

He made it to his office. As he bent over and picked up *The Philadelphia Inquirer*, he had a flashback to three weeks earlier when he picked up the paper and read the article about the trial in Arkansas for the ownership of a slave. The article changed his life.

Once again, he unlocked the door and turned the sign around where it said "Open". The writing on the door said "Caleb Matthews, Attorney at Law, Esq". He took the paper and started into his office, where he noticed a large stack of letters in the mail bin.

He was sorting through the mail when he saw the letter from the Matthews Plantation with his mother's handwriting on the envelope. When he got to his desk, the letter Charlotte had mentioned in her note was laying on his desk. He still didn't understand why the letter was at the office and the note was on the dining room table.

He opened the letter from his mother and began reading. It was a litany of questions. "Did you see Zeek?" was the first question. It was followed by a continuous line of questioning from, "How tall was he?" to, "Did he recognize you?"

Caleb finished reading the questions and then was shocked when he read, "I've been sharing your letters with Missy for several years."

He stopped reading and looked toward the street. The wind was blowing a steady flow of leaves toward the north. The warm southern wind and the sun that he enjoyed while walking to the office was going to change to rain clouds. He could see the clouds building as he looked out into the street. Noticing the leaves and the clouds gave his mind a chance to recover from finding out his mother had read his letters with Missy "for years".

"Your dad read the letter about your trip to Arkansas, and also the newspaper article," she had written. "We sat on the veranda with Missy and we all talked about your trip to Arkansas."

The writings of his mother had gotten his full attention.

Caleb finished reading the letter. He was shocked when they told him how sorry they were that he had not spent his life with Missy and the boys. He was more shocked when she had written, "Your dad considers Missy his daughter-in-law now that we have found Zeek."

Caleb opened Charlotte's letter. He read through her expressions of disbelief that he had not told her about Ross and Zeek. She said she was so hurt by the news that she needed to spend more time in St. Louis before she came back to Philadelphia. It was a cold letter. Caleb read through it twice more and noticed Charlotte never referred to Zeek or their children. It was just about her and how embarrassed she was to think she had been married to a man for over thirty years that fathered children by a slave.

Caleb left his desk and went next door to the coffee shop. He got a cup of coffee and a pastry.

The wind he had watched blowing leaves was now bringing a slight mist into his face. The little raindrops were refreshing. It was what Caleb needed to clear his mind.

He had not unrolled the newspaper. He did not open any of the letters from his clients. He also ignored the one from the clerk of the court labeled "ruling enclosed". His mind was caught somewhere between his son, Zeek Matthews, and the news he had gotten from his mother in her letter. He was astonished when he got to Arkansas and found Zeek Matthews, a slave, had lived as a free man and was married to a Choctaw maiden. He was now just as astonished by the change of attitude of his parents, Donald and Francis Matthews.

Caleb thought about the trip and all that he learned in Arkansas. After he read the newspaper article giving details about a court case in which the Reynolds Plantation had tried to reclaim him as their property, he had been anxious to see if the newspaper article was accurate.

He had read in the newspaper article where Ross, his other son, was the key witness proving Zeek was a slave.

Caleb thought about what had happened since he left to investigate the newspaper story. When he got to Arkansas, beginning with the time he spent in Cotter Arkansas in a hotel, he had listened to stories about the trial for the ownership of Zeek. He listened to the excitement in a man's voice as he told Caleb how Mr. Hayes had stopped the court case and bought Zeek's freedom. He listened to the description of the emotion that filled the courtroom while Mr. Hayes counted out the $2000 for Zeek's freedom.

Caleb meant the sheriff when he got to the courthouse in Marshall, Arkansas. He could still see the expression on the Searcy County Sheriff's face when he introduced himself as Zeek's father and wanted directions to Zeek's house. He thought about Sheriff Kirk's offer to drive him to Zeek's house. He thought about the excitement, and how he would never forget the reunion with his son.

Caleb sat down at his desk. He decided he would write his mother first. He would not write Charlotte until later. He had no idea what he wanted to say to her. He understood her being shocked to find out he had a couple of boys born while he was a boy still living on the Matthews Plantation in Alabama.

He began the letter to his mother.

"Dear Mother, I don't know how to start this letter. I got to meet Zeek. He is now Zeek Matthews, a free man living in Searcy County Arkansas. For two weeks, people came to his house to meet his dad. At first it was awkward. I couldn't adjust to the life that he lives. It's a simple life. He has a cabin in a beautiful setting. His best friend, Jim Campbell, who he left the survey with, lives about twenty-five feet away in another cabin. He has shared his life with the most beautiful maiden I've ever seen. Vida is—" Caleb stopped writing. He had never thought about describing Vida, Zeek's wife.

"Vida's mind is uncluttered," Caleb wrote and then went on to describe how she never discussed a problem. "She did not tell me how she and Zeek got together. She never mentioned how she learned to speak Zeek's language. She also has learned to read and write. She's active in their church. She is part of the little school in the community."

Caleb stopped. While he was writing about his trip to Arkansas, he had forgotten almost all the things he read about Missy and the new relationship she had developed with his parents.

Caleb stopped writing about the family. He addressed the next few lines to his dad. He wrote about how hot the argument was becoming between the free states and the slave states. He wrote about how he was at the southern tip of the free states in Philadelphia. He knew the struggle would come to a head. And then he wrote that he would be back to the plantation as soon as he could. He did not mention any anticipated interruption of their lives by a Civil War.

CHAPTER 13

After reading the letter from Caleb, along with the newspaper article describing how Zeek had gained his freedom in Arkansas, Donald Matthews could wait no longer. He was going to get Ross and return him to the Matthews Plantation. He was also his grandson, and deserved freedom just as much as Zeek.

It had been three days since he left to go to Mississippi. He was making the trip with two of his most trusted servants and riding in his best carriage, which was being pulled by the fastest team of horses the Matthews Plantation owned.

While he was traveling to the Reynolds Plantation, he passed several other plantations before he got to Mississippi. He recognized some of the names and was acquainted with their owners. He finally passed the sign for the Reynolds Plantation and stopped at the first buildings to inquire about the headquarters. He was anxious to see his old college friend and fraternity brother. He was sure that Joseph Reynolds did nothing wrong when he let Zeek and Ross join the survey crew.

When he inquired at the first complex of the Reynolds Plantation, he was told the main house was still a full day's travel. He stopped twice more at building complexes which were bigger than the entire Matthews Plantation headquarters. He was told neither of those were the main headquarters but the main house was still farther into Mississippi. He began to wonder how large the Reynolds plantation actually was. He finally arrived at the headquarters.

He drove the buggy up a lane with magnolia trees on each side. He saw the plantation home with three full stories and the veranda around each floor. There were columns spaced equally around the entire building extending from the ground to the bottom of the roof above the veranda on the top floor.

He was greeted by a well-dressed black gentleman at the gate.

"I am Donald Matthews, from Alabama. I have come to see Joseph," he told the butler.

He was told to wait and Mr. Reynolds would be there shortly. He sat there, observing the plantation house and the surrounding buildings. While he wasn't aggressive with expanding his holdings at the Matthews Plantation, it appeared that his fraternity brother had a different management plan entirely.

After a very short wait, the well-dressed black man returned with a man some thirty years younger than Donald Matthews.

"I am here to see Joseph Reynolds," he said as he introduced himself. "I am Donald Matthews. We were fraternity brothers when we were in college, and I operate the Matthews Plantation in Alabama."

"I am Joseph Reynolds Junior," the short fellow introduced himself. He was dressed in a white suit and was wearing a wide-brimmed Panama hat. After a short pause, he answered, "My father has been dead now for over a year."

After expressing his condolences, Donald stated the purpose of his visit.

"Almost forty years ago, I took two young men to New Orleans and your dad took possession of them," Donald Matthews described the transfer of Ross and Zeek to the Reynolds Plantation.

The young man's eyes widened as he exclaimed, "You're the grandfather of Ross and Zeek!"

Donald Matthews said, "I am here to take Ross back to Alabama".

The discussion of the ownership of "the boys" became intense. Donald Matthews made it clear his intention was to take his grandson back to Alabama. The young Mr. Reynolds was equally adamant that Ross was his property.

Donald Matthews was traveling with two of his most trusted servants. The young men had been taught to read and write and were capable of managing the plantation. They bristled when the young Mr. Reynolds spoke so strongly about Ross and Zeek.

They retrieved a copy of the original paper transferring Ross and Zeek to the Reynolds Plantation. They read the line that stated "it is the option of the Matthews Plantation to retain ownership and remove either or both of the young black men described in this paper as Ross and Zeek and return them to the Matthews Plantation".

They read further, where the contract stated, "Mr. Reynolds must never reveal where the two young men came from nor may he abuse them in any treatment whatsoever."

After the contract was read, both servants and Donald Matthews restated almost simultaneously the purpose of their trip. "We have come for Ross and we are taking him home."

The weather warmed up considerably during the time they started their journey back to Alabama. The sky was bright blue. The warm sun felt good to the passengers in the carriage as it rolled smoothly along after leaving the Reynolds Plantation. Ross was sitting in the backseat with his grandfather, Donald Matthews.

All of the intense discussion ended before he was brought to the front of the mansion at the Reynolds Plantation. After the terms of the contract were read, the young Reynolds protested that he was never advised that the contract existed and he wasn't sure he would abide by it.

Donald Matthews did not raise his voice, but he informed Joseph Reynolds Junior that he was leaving the plantation, going back to Alabama, and his grandson Ross would be accompanying him.

Ross got there just as Donald Matthews agreed to send two slaves to the New Orleans auction in exchange for Ross. The Reynolds Plantation would have the option to either pick up the payment or the slaves. Joseph Reynolds Junior insisted they be healthy, not over thirty years old, and of good size. Donald Ross agreed. He was willing to give anything for the return of Ross.

When the carriage left, Ross had no luggage or any personal possessions. Donald Matthews did not question his lack of belongings.

"Do you remember me?" he finally asked Ross after they had been traveling for almost an hour.

Ross did not look at Mr. Matthews. He stared away into the distance before he answered, "Yes, sir."

Ross's mind was racing back to the hotel in New Orleans. While he was riding in the back of the carriage with Donald Matthews, his grandfather, he remembered all too well watching him walk away, leaving him and Zeek at the hotel.

"What's going to happen to me now?" Ross asked his grandfather.

Donald Matthews began an attempt to explain how sorry he was for what happened. Ross sat and listened. Donald Matthews did not mention he knew Ross had been to Searcy County Arkansas and testified in a trial for the freedom of Zeek. He never mentioned the letter Caleb had written. He did not mention all the changes taking place at the Matthews Plantation.

"We are going to see your mother, Missy," he finally answered. "She will take care of you and you will be all right."

Donald Matthews felt awkward trying to explain to a man in his late forties how life was going to change. He was returning to the plantation where he was born. He tried to visualize Zeek and the way he was described as a successful family man with his freedom.

He was almost brought to tears when he looked at Ross. Ross appeared to be in good health, but his hands were bruised and worn from the work he had been doing. His shoes were in tatters. They were barely hanging on his feet, and should have been replaced a long while ago. His pant legs were uneven, with one of the legs much shorter than the other. He had a gallus running across his left shoulder and tied on the right side of the front and in the back of the pants. There were no pockets in the pants.

Donald Matthews stared at the countryside of

Mississippi. The fields were ragged. There were some where the cotton had not been picked. It was November, and the cotton should've been picked before the end of October. He would be proud when he got Ross out of Mississippi. He began to make plans, but he stopped in mid-thought.

"When I get Ross home, I will leave it up to Missy and Mrs. Matthews," he decided. He looked at Ross and tried to envision what they would do for him.

CHAPTER 14

It was early December in Alabama. All the leaves had fallen from the elm and sycamore trees. The oak trees were brown but still had their leaves, while the live oaks had taken on the deeper purplish-green for their winter leaves.

Missy had just finished a jacket. She was making clothes for Ross. She had enjoyed measuring him to fit the jacket.

She became overjoyed every time she thought about the day he arrived back from Mississippi. She was walking between the kitchen and the main house when she saw the carriage coming.

Mrs. Matthews had told her several days earlier that Donald was gone to the Reynolds Plantation to bring Ross "home". Even after being told that, she was not prepared for the excitement of seeing Ross sitting in the carriage as they pulled into the yard.

Missy did not remember running to the carriage. She just remembered seeing the top of Ross's head. Her memory of his hair and the complexion of his skin and the look in his eyes seem to carry her to the carriage. She remembered climbing on the carriage. She must have jumped on top of Ross and started hugging him and kissing the top of his head.

Ross had sat on the carriage and returned her hugs, but actually never said anything through his tears.

Now, that was almost a month ago. There had been a lot of discussion. Caleb had actually written another letter before Mr. Matthews returned with Ross.

"What are the plans for Ross?" was the first line in Caleb's letter. Missy had opened the letter. Mrs. Matthews had walked into the kitchen holding the envelope in front of her. When she reached the table where Missy was starting to mix the bread for the day, she laid the envelope in front of Missy.

Missy was startled. She had never had a letter placed in front of her to open before. She read the address and it was to: Mrs. Francis Matthews. Matthews Plantation followed, with the route number for delivery. She looked at the lower left corner of the envelope and saw "Missy" underlined twice.

She had opened the letter and was too nervous

to read it. She handed the letter back to Mrs. Matthews after reading the first line. She followed Mrs. Matthews into the parlor. Donald Matthews joined them. Ross had been sent on an errand by Mr. Matthews and was not there as the letter was being read.

"The day's coming when slavery will end," Caleb had written in his letter. "The argument will not end with the free states insisting on the slave's freedom, it will end when the slaves realize they are people." Missy listened as those lines from Caleb's letter were read.

But today Missy was too happy to worry about who owned who or what. She was enjoying life. She was being treated respectfully. She sometimes wondered if her treatment was more of a repentance for the past than actual appreciation for the present.

Missy thought about the letter as she continued to work on a pair of pants for Ross. She had started the pants before she decided to make the jacket. This was the third pair of pants she had made for him since he arrived back at the plantation.

Donald Matthews had gone through the stock of shoes until he found a pair he thought was right for Ross.

Missy remembered the day he found the shoes. She had watched him take the old pants Ross was wearing and the tattered shoes to the burn pile. The pile was where they burned all the unwanted things. They always used the ashes for areas in the garden. She watched as Mr. Matthews made sure the shoes and the pants burned up completely.

Missy had wondered what was going through his mind as she watched. Was he trying to destroy the evidence of the condition Ross was in when he arrived at the plantation?

There was too much going on in Missy's life in the past few months for her to understand completely. She was still the property of the Matthews Plantation. Ross had returned, and he also was the property of Matthews Plantation. Missy felt relieved and proud when Ross arrived home, but she was disappointed as she watched Mr. Matthews load two slaves for the trip to the auction in New Orleans. She found out as they were leaving, they were part of the trade to bring Ross back home.

Ross came in and interrupted her while she was working on the pants.

"Let's go sit on the porch." Ross would never refer to the veranda as a veranda. It was a porch.

Missy stopped working on the pants and picked up a container of tea, along with two cups, and followed Ross to the veranda.

She poured the tea. After they had taken a few sips and while Missy was staring toward the live oak tree, Ross posed a question.

"What should I call you?" he asked.

Missy was shocked by the question. When she thought about it though she realized he had not called her anything since he came home.

"What do you want to call me?" she finally returned his question with a question.

"Was it Mums, or was it Mom?' Ross asked another question. And then he added, "I don't remember."

They sat in silence for several minutes as their minds tried to retrace the time before he was taken away to the Reynolds Plantation. The sun was beginning to set, and the shadow of the live oak tree was nearing the veranda.

They had not answered the question.

CHAPTER 15

The war between the states—the southern rebellion—the northern aggression—whatever name they chose to call it—was eight years of turmoil. There was not much activity on the plantation. The rumblings of the Civil War a few years earlier had culminated with shots being fired at Fort Sumter in South Carolina.

Missy had just gotten used to Ross being back at the plantation when the war started. In Alabama, it was the northern aggression. When Caleb wrote his last letter before the battle at Fort Sumter, he called it the southern rebellion.

Donald Matthews was buried shortly after the war ended. His grave was at the edge of the canopy of the live oak tree. They cut off one of the limbs to make room for his grave. Six months before his passing, he had chosen the spot. He said, "I want to be far enough away from the veranda and still be close enough to be where the boys used to play under the tree".

He told Missy, "The memory I cherish most is watching Zeek and Ross after I realized they belonged to Caleb," and then he stopped. With a tremor in his voice, he would continue, "the saddest day was the day I took them away."

Missy slowly rocked her chair. It was past teatime, and Mrs. Matthews was asleep in her chair. Mrs. Matthews entered her seventh decade about the time the Civil War started in 1861. She would reminisce about the way things were before the war with Missy. But this morning, she drank coffee and started to take a nap without much conversation.

Missy listened to the soft sound of Mrs. Matthews breathing. Missy sometimes got lost in her thoughts about the years she had spent with Mrs. Matthews.

She remembered going for walks with her and Caleb when she was about five years old. She had never developed an understanding of their relationship. It had just been a relationship without promises, and it still was. Missy's mother was responsible for the kitchen duties before Missy took over the kitchen. Missy had performed those duties for the Matthews family for over fifty years.

Missy knew she was no longer a slave. She

knew when the war ended, she was a free woman. She had stayed where she was. She still cooked every morning. But since Mr. Matthews' passing, she only cooked for four people: herself, Mrs. Matthews, and the caretakers of the house. The grounds of the plantation had not changed much. There was still the separate kitchen with the covered walkway joining the kitchen to the house. The parlor, the large dining hall. And the entry with two stairways. And of course, the veranda.

The Matthews Plantation was not burned out during the war. Most of the battles were fought along the southern coast near Mobile, or they had been in the northern part of the state. There had never been any reason to destroy Donald Matthews property. Missy wondered if Caleb knew people who kept the war away from his family.

"Missy, why did you let me fall asleep?" Mrs. Matthews was awake.

"You looked too peaceful for me to wake you up," Missy answered.

"I dreamed about Caleb," Mrs. Matthews said. "I never dream in the daytime."

Missy didn't ask about Mrs. Matthews' dream. She was always telling Missy after Mr. Matthews died that she had dreamed about Caleb coming home.

Caleb came to visit just before the war started, and he spent time on the veranda with Ross and his dad, Mr. Matthews. Missy was there a few minutes during their visit with Caleb, but didn't have any part in the conversation.

"It was too hard to try to talk to him," she answered Mrs. Matthews' question after Caleb left.

There wasn't much communication during the war. Missy read maybe three letters Caleb wrote to his mother. She did notice in one letter that he told his mother Charlotte was spending most of her time in St. Louis. "She has never gotten over me having the boys with Missy," he had written.

Missy's understanding of life was no broader than her experience of living on the Matthews Plantation. Now, over sixty years later, she was a free woman—but her life was shaped when she was born half Choctaw and half black, with a mother who was a slave and a cook in the plantation kitchen.

Missy had gained standing within the Matthews family. When the census was taken by the new governor after the war ended, she was listed as Missy Matthews. A free woman and residing at the Matthews Plantation. Mrs. Matthews told the person doing the survey of individuals that she was a member of the Matthews family.

Ross was now in charge of the sharecroppers. He was living in one of the plantation farmhouses where Mr. Matthews allowed him to live shortly after he came back from the Reynolds Plantation.

Ross had a wife. Missy was not aware of her until Ross brought her to the plantation while Caleb was there for one of his visits.

Mrs. Matthews had whispered, "I think she's a

runaway from the Reynolds Plantation."

While Mrs. Matthews was taking her nap, Missy had laughed when she thought about when Mrs. Matthews told her she thought Ross's woman was a runaway slave.

"Missy, are you going to cook any lunch?" Mrs. Matthews asked.

Missy was always amazed at Mrs. Matthews' appetite for food. By the time breakfast was finished, she was ready to discuss what food was next.

"I don't know, do we need lunch?" Missy always liked to ask that because she knew what the answer was going to be.

"Sure," Mrs. Matthews would always say, and Missy would come up with something, and she would always eat it heartily.

"Caleb is coming home," Mrs. Matthews said, without referring back to her dream.

"How would you know that?" Missy asked.

"I just do." She paused. "Maybe it's a mother's instinct."

Missy left the veranda. She went into the pantry portion of the kitchen and began trying to decide what would be the easiest lunch. She started to mix the batter for Johnny cakes, and she would cook some early greens to go with them. She started boiling two eggs, not knowing what this lunch was going to be.

A new era was beginning at the Matthews Plantation.

CHAPTER 16

Missy watched from the kitchen window as Caleb walked circles underneath the live oak tree. She watched him as he walked to the spot where they always sat and played when they were kids.

She thought for a minute he was going to sit down in the dirt. She watched him, remembering when they were kids, but they were now almost seventy years old.

For just a moment, after staring at Caleb, she imagined a flashback. "Missy come see what I found," she remembered him saying. She watched as he began kicking in the dirt. The memory was from sixty years earlier. In her mind, the sound was like it was only yesterday.

She thought back to the letter he had written Mrs. Matthews a few weeks earlier. It was only a few days after Mrs. Matthews woke up from her nap and declared, "Caleb is coming home."

"Missy, I am writing this letter to you," the letter began. "Mother is not making much sense in her letters."

Caleb went on to describe the things his mother had written to him. It was a jumble of things, some she had imagined, and others even if they were true, Caleb wondered if it was possible.

"She is still upset that I didn't come home when dad died," Caleb wrote. "I didn't get the letter until almost a month after he passed away."

The restoration of the railroad and the communication by telegraph was complete. During the war, the Union Army maintained several railroads for their use. The Confederacy did not have enough communication to support their troops and they were never able to control any of the railroads.

The old plantations throughout the South, including the Matthews Plantation, were still not served by a railroad or telegraph. The mail service was poor, as most people were using the telegraph for communication.

Caleb was afraid to send any mail or any other communication back to the plantation during the war.

He was now comfortable with writing and travel, but Mrs. Matthews had not forgiven him for the years he had not stayed in touch.

Missy had become comfortable talking to Caleb, and would sit and visit with him on the veranda since he came home. She could not explain her feelings toward him. She loved him so much when the boys were born and she believed he would stand up and be a part of her life.

She had never gotten over the disappointment of him leaving, and she had emotional scars left from the time she was alone after the boys were taken away. She had suffered through loneliness and depression.

She was sustained emotionally by her relationship with Mrs. Matthews. Now she was spending her time with Caleb because Mrs. Matthews was becoming unable to stay active and communicate.

Missy would go to the kitchen at her usual time and begin cooking each morning. The caretakers of the house would come and tell her when Mrs. Matthews would get out of bed.

Mrs. Matthews got up early every day when Caleb first arrived. She lost interest in their conversations when she realized Caleb could not relate to the happenings during the time of his absence. She was thrilled to talk about Ross and Zeek. She got excited when Caleb told her about his trips to Arkansas to see Zeek. Caleb made several trips to Arkansas and visited with Zeek and his wife, Vida.

Missy got a letter from Vida. She had written a

long letter detailing the story of the years she and Zeek had been together. She wrote about when Zeek and Jim Campbell left the survey and joined her and her sister. She wrote about Zeek's anxiety during the trial for his freedom. It was hard for Missy to comprehend the amount of time Vida's letter covered.

Missy suddenly realized after reading the names of every family member listed by Vida that she had grandchildren and even great-grandchildren living in Searcy County Arkansas. Family she had never seen. Vida made no promises to ever come to Alabama. She didn't ask Missy to travel to Arkansas.

Missy gave Vida's letter to Caleb. She sat quietly and watched Caleb as he read the letter. It was one of the mornings when Mrs. Matthews stayed in bed.

Missy had eaten breakfast in the parlor with Caleb.

"I'm not going back to Philadelphia," Caleb declared halfway through the breakfast meal.

Missy did not respond. She had never asked anything about Charlotte. She knew from reading Caleb's letters in the past that Charlotte had moved to St. Louis.

"You're going to live here?" Missy had asked.

"Some of the time," Caleb answered, and then he added, "I am going to spend a lot of time in Arkansas."

Caleb finished the meal and they moved to the

veranda. Missy brought two cups of coffee, along with another letter from Vida.

After Caleb finished rereading Vida's letter, he asked, "Have you ever heard of this place in Arkansas called Big Flat?"

Missy answered, "Yes."

She told Caleb about Ross telling her Big Flat was the last place he saw Zeek. It was the last time he saw him before he went to Arkansas to testify. It was where they had been camped.

"Ross described it as being almost a perfect place," Missy went on with her story. "I think it was because they had been so miserable in the swamps of Arkansas with the snakes and the mosquitoes."

Caleb stood up. He walked to the end of the veranda. It reminded Missy of what Mr. Matthews would always do. After standing there for a minute, Caleb turned back around, facing Missy.

"I went to that place the last time I went to see Zeek," Caleb said and then returned to his chair and sat back down.

"Well?" Missy's tone made it a question for Caleb to answer.

"I don't know," Caleb paused. "It was really hot the day I was there last year/"

Caleb took a couple of sips of his coffee. Missy sat, waiting for him to continue. She remembered how slow and deliberate he was with his conversation years earlier. She just waited. She knew he would continue when he was ready.

"I got bit by the chiggers and the ticks." Caleb sounded irritable, and then he continued, "I wasn't happy."

Missy ignored him. Vida wrote in one of her letters about this little red bug that would bite you. She said it was so small you could barely see it. Missy didn't remember the name of it, but she was sure it was the chigger based on Caleb's description of his bites.

The day ended. When Missy finally went to Mrs. Matthews, she was alert, feeling good, and asking what was for dinner. Life was normal at the Matthews Plantation.

CHAPTER 17

The main house at the Matthews Plantation had become the headquarters for managing the sharecroppers. A large portion of the original land owned by the plantation was sold to get capital to continue the operations of the remaining property.

Most of the land sold was never farmed for cotton or tobacco. All the mules and other farm animals were no longer kept at the compound next to the main house. They were moved out to each individual sharecropper according to the number they needed for their farming operations. When Caleb came back from Philadelphia to live on the plantation, he spent several days going over the property with Ross and checking on each one of the sharecroppers.

After he finished visiting with the sharecroppers, he was spending an afternoon sitting on the veranda with Missy. He began describing all the things he saw while he was inspecting the plantation and visiting with the former slaves. For the most part, the sharecroppers were part of the Matthews Plantation long before they got their freedom.

"All of the farmers were here before I left, and most of them are either a grandson or a great-grandson of the original slaves who were here before Mom and Dad were married and took over the plantation." Caleb stopped and thought for a minute. "They all told me their last name was 'Matthews'." Caleb caught his breath and looked away from Missy for a moment.

"Missy, that will not work." His voice was stern. "You are a Matthews, I am a Matthews. Ross and Zeek have got to be Matthews. All the rest of them—" He never finished his sentence.

They sat in silence. After a few minutes, he added, "I am proud they want to use my name, I am just not going to have it."

Missy was trying to make sense of what Caleb said. She had been signing her name as Missy Matthews ever since the population census after the war. It was Caleb's mother who gave her the name when she answered the census taker who was doing the update for the population records.

Mr. Matthews furnished a description of all the

slaves and the number living on the plantation. After the records were updated, he signed an affidavit of the accuracy of the report. He did this just before he passed away, after the war ended. He also verified the slaves were no longer the property of the plantation and were now free to leave if they chose to.

Caleb was amazed by the change in responsibility the slaves were taking by becoming their own boss and farming on a sharecrop basis. He knew Ross was giving them all the help possible for them to succeed. It would determine how successful the plantation was, and the former slaves if they were able to convert to freedom.

"Missy, how do you suddenly take over your life when it's been someone else's responsibility?" Caleb asked

Missy remembered her frustration with the question. She also recalled when all the other slaves left their quarters to go out into the plantation and become sharecroppers. There were family units which existed and no one was aware of the relationships. Missy watched as one woman claimed her four children from the slaves, and also left with their father. They were a family. She had been a field worker who rode the wagon each day out into the field to work. The man was a keeper of the mules and the farm equipment. He was skilled at keeping the mules shod. The children were not old enough to have duties assigned to them yet. They left as a family and were no longer in the possession of Matthews Plantation. They were now independent sharecroppers.

Missy wondered how quickly they would adapt to cooking and providing for themselves. They ate in the slave kitchen and lived in the slave quarters. They would no longer be eating the food cooked in the huge pots and the bread cooked in the kitchen. Missy was thinking about the changes she had made since they left the plantation headquarters.

Caleb continued his discussion of the plantation. Missy spent the time thinking about the change and didn't really listen to what he was saying. She was amazed that he felt the need to involve her in the decisions, but she agreed with him when he didn't want everyone to be called by their last name.

"How many of them do you remember?" Missy asked Caleb.

After thinking for a minute, Caleb answered, "Some."

After Missy asked the question, Caleb spent the next few minutes trying to remember what his duties were before he was sent away to Dartmouth.

"Do you remember what I was supposed to do before I left for college?" he asked Missy.

"No, I don't," she answered. "I just remember I ran errands for the kitchen and did things for your mother."

They both spent a few minutes trying to remember what their chores were.

"After we started—" Missy stopped herself

before she said anything about their intimacy. Her face flushed and she looked away toward the live oak tree. She tried to remember how old they were back then.

"This is not good," Caleb said. "It's bringing back memories of times we left behind long ago." He laughed. After a moment, he asked Missy, "How old were we then?"

She didn't answer. He asked another question. "How old are we now?"

"Too old," Missy answered, and changed the subject to how many kids Zeek had.

"He has a boy and a girl," Caleb answered. "They are almost fifty years old. I believe they are 50 years old..." He began to count up how many grandchildren Zeek had. He finally arrived at the number of five. He told Missy, "We've got two or three great-grandchildren living in Arkansas".

Missy got out of her chair and started into the house, leaving the veranda. "I'll go get Vida's letter." She paused as she went through the door into the house. "She listed everyone of them, and I think she gives their ages."

Missy returned with the letter, and they spent quite a bit of their time on the veranda re-reading it.

After reading Vida's list of the grandchildren and great-grandchildren, Caleb and Missy read the description she gave about Zeek's attachment to Big Flat. She wrote about how it was a special place to both of them. It was where Zeek decided to leave the survey and start a life with her. She wrote about how much they enjoyed going to the trading post and walking over the grounds where the camp was. She described the spring and the water flowing past the buildings which were built where the survey camp was located. From her description, the place was an inspiration to both of them.

Missy and Caleb enjoyed reading about Big Flat. They were also trying to get a picture of Zeek and Vida's life in their mind.

After they finished their discussion of all the children and grandchildren Zeek had in Arkansas, Caleb suggested they go for a walk around the plantation house.

During the time Caleb had been back at the plantation, it was the most time he had spent with Missy. He had tried to avoid contact with her because Charlotte was in St. Louis and he was still married.

This discussion was not helpful. Even though they were in their early seventies, the old flames from years ago started to reignite while they were sitting on the veranda. They had never even touched hands since he had come home. When they started down the veranda, Caleb went off the steps first and stopped. Missy was looking toward the live oak tree and did not see him until she ran into him. Caleb caught her. When he lifted her up to keep her from falling, it was the first time they had looked directly into each other's eyes.

Missy took his arm, and they started to walk around the house. They reached the spot underneath the live oak tree where they had played years before. Caleb began to kick the dirt. They both spotted it at the same time. A black onyx locket with the chain missing was exposed in the dirt. Missy almost dove to get it. She stood up with the locket in the palm of her hand and looked at Caleb.

They did not say a word. It was a locket from years ago, which Caleb had taken from his mother's jewelry box. Missy had worn it inside her dress where it could not be seen. They were looking at a token he had given her before Zeek was born.

They walked slowly away from the oak tree. They remained silent until they reached the back of the covered walkway connecting the kitchen to the main house.

Caleb finally spoke, barely above a whisper. "What are we going to do now?"

Missy's mind was racing as she tried to figure out what they should do when they were a couple who had lost a lot of years for reasons beyond their control.

"I want to go to Arkansas," she finally answered.

"We will meet all the kids listed in the letter." Caleb made a declaration.

A new day had arrived. A new day that started with no more plans than when they were children before the boys were born. They began to plan a trip without discussing it with anyone. They left the plantation, going to Montgomery, Alabama to catch a train.

They spent two days shopping in Montgomery. Missy Matthews was going on a journey with Caleb Matthews.

Missy watched Caleb walking toward her while she waited to board the train. Very little about Caleb's appearance resembled the young man who fathered their children. While she was happy with their new relationship, she knew their lives together would never be nor could be what she dreamed of when the boys were born. It wasn't a matter of age, it was a matter of circumstances. While she was still beautiful with the same skin tone she inherited from her Choctaw father, her dreams of a life with Caleb were in the past. Caleb was affectionate and was treating her well but Missy was bothered by his marriage and the years he had deserted her. However, she was ready to move on as part of his life. She was ready to start a relationship with their children and their grandchildren. She would ride the train to Arkansas.

"When we get to Arkansas, I want to go to Big Flat," she said as they boarded the train.

"Why would we want to do that?" Caleb asked.

"It's where Zeek chose freedom. I want to be at Big Flat with him, when he realizes I am free, too," Missy answered.

Missy sat next to the window as the train pulled away from the station. She heard the train blowing its whistle.

She thought it was the sound of freedom. She was a mother. She was a grandmother. She was a great-grandmother. She was sitting next to the man with whom she started it all when they were children.

Missy Matthews, a slave no more.

ABOUT THE AUTHOR

Sam Pemberton was born on Bratton Creek, at an old homestead that hadn't changed much since the pioneer days. The year was 1944. Pemberton graduated from Big Flat high school. After their graduation in 1962, Sam married the love of his life, Patricia Treat.

He has worked construction in the drywall trade for most of his life. Sam presently lives in the beautiful Ozarks and continues in construction. He loves writing his stories and enjoys his morning coffee and porch time.

OTHER BOOKS BY SAM PEMBERTON

The Moonshiner and the Preacher
Finding Big Flat
Zeek's Journey to Freedom
Livin' Under Goldies Rule